The Family Reunion

A Fictional Family Portrait

of

Not-So-Real

Family Members

The Family Reunion

A Fictional Family Portrait
of
Not-So-Real
Family Members

by

Richard M. Grove

Hidden Brook Press

Third Edition

Hidden Brook Press
www.HiddenBrookPress.com
writers@HiddenBrookPress.com

The Family Reunion
by Richard M. Grove

Layout and Design – Richard M. Grove
Cover Design – Richard M. Grove
Cover Photograph – Richard M. Grove
Editor – Kimberley E. Grove

Printed and bound in Canada

Library and Archives Canada Cataloguing in Publication

Grove, Richard M. (Richard Marvin), 1953–
The family reunion : a fictional family portrait of not-so-real
family members / by Richard M. Grove. – 3rd ed.

Short stories.
ISBN 978-1-897475-35-5

I. Title.

PS8563.R75F35 2010 C813'.54 C2010-904552-1

This book is dedicated to:

The Grove,
Sherman
and Hunt Family.

Find yourself
in one or more of these characters.

I have hidden you in characters
you might not, at first, think to look.
You are all there.

Thank you **Bill Hunt**

for your attentive

red ink.

Thank you **R.D. Roy / Doogla,**

mi hermano,

for your editorial guidance

and **Jennifer Footman**

for your input.

Most of all,

thank you,

Kim,

my darling wife,

for your loving patience and

support of my creative spirit

and for all of the practical

assistance you give me.

Dear Reader:

I am proud that this book has had a number of printings and is now in its third edition with some corrections, some character developments and even a brand new character. I wonder if I will ever finish this book.

This book is primarily a collection of vignettes, character sketches, that are strung together in and around a family reunion. Find yourself in each of these characters not in just one. I have purposefully used many names from my family and friends but in no way should a single character be thought of as a portrayal of reality let alone a single individual. Stories and personal characteristics that I see in myself and in others are simply the launching platform for these characters buried between truth and fiction.

Most often a character in the story is not even remotely like a person in real life but sometimes a person has simply been renamed. In most situations my own personal experiences and traits are sprinkled throughout all of the characters, including the dead chicken and the hooker. I wonder what Sigmund Freud would say about the inevitability of this.

Richard M. Grove

Family Members:

The Family Reunion

Welcome

Welcome to my family. Mostly we are a close-knit bunch, all living within five miles of each other. We get together at each other's places for dinners, to help paint each other's houses or build a shed. Sometimes we bring in the crops together or just sit on the front porch on a hot summer evening complaining about the price of gas or seed for next year's crops. Like every-one we complain about how many trucks there are on the highways or how the kids just aren't very polite these days. Mostly we try to stay away from topics like politics and religion. Ma says, "There's no point in getting the blood to boilin'." We were taught that family doesn't quarrel over differences. Mind you, there would be plenty of room for scrapping if we got started. Ma and Pa have been voting Progressive Conservative all of their lives. All us kids were weaned on Conservative rallies from before we could even walk. I still vote conservative but some of the black sheep of the family swung over to the Liberal party some time ago. Ma's motto is that we leave politics at the front door with the muddy boots.

Despite how often we get together the one thing that we always do is gather at least once a year for a family reunion. Some years, if someone gets us organized in the summer, the family reunion is out at my cousins, David and Marilyn's, cottages near Turkey Point on Lake Erie. It is a long drive through tobacco country 'before you get to a single, slow lane that winds you past clusters of modest, but well kept, cottages until you arrive under ancient maples to park on the grass in front of a large, low slung deck. There has been many a family reunion out there.

Some years we get together at Ma and Pa's farm. They live in a mid-1800 stone house on

100 acres of rolling hills near Puslinch out a ways between Hamilton and Kitchener. When arriving there you would slow for the turn off the dusty gravel road, drive between two monolithic stone pillars, up the long sumach lined lane and arrive at their grand grey stone house. Their house looks over golden pastures and orchards for many a mile. The view is stupendous all year long. From season to season you are met with the glory God gave us.

Even if someone gets us organized in the summer we still rent a country hall near Ancaster in the winter about Christmas time. This old one-room-school-come-community-hall echoes a hundred years of country tradition that takes me back to my childhood. It has a big old kitchen for getting the food ready and a plentiful sized hall for setting up tables and letting the kids run.

Christmas in the old schoolhouse is fine and all, but me, I was bucking for a new tradition. I wanted to have a Christmas family reunion somewhere exotic like Cuba one year. As soon as I made the suggestion someone said lets go to Las Vegas instead, another said Florida. Someone said they couldn't get that much time off work and another said "Who is gunna milk my dang cows if I'm tannin' on some beach?" I guess I just have to come to terms with the notion that I'm not going to get my country-rooted family much past the bend in the highway let alone off the continent. I figure they are a home-bound bunch for the most part and nothing much is going to change that. They don't want to venture out much past the front gate if they can avoid it. A trip to the post office and the grocery store once a week is all that most of them ever do day after day, year after year.

Probably, most of them have never traveled past Niagara Falls or had a tan on their legs or much down past their red necks since they were ten. With horror, my imagination pictures the bunch of them walking up to the front desk of a fancy Cuban hotel still wearing their galoshes and their green John Deer caps. "Do you-o have-o our reservations for-o our family-o of thirty-two, sinyor-o." Maybe it is best if we just have Christmas in Ancaster every year. I might not recognize Ma and Pa with sand between their toes anyway.

Pretty much everyone comes to our family reunions near every year. Ma and Pa haven't ever missed one. I missed going once when I had a summer job flipping burgers and makin' greasy fries at the chip wagon in Cayuga. Another time, I was on my way with a watermelon under my arm but I got talking to Janny, a pretty girl from Ancaster. She had long blond hair that flowed down her back like angel wings. I sat rocking back and forth on that watermelon talking and talking with her until it finally burst right from under me. We both pretty near peed ourselves laughing; tears streamed down our faces for the longest time. I plum forgot all about the family reunion until it was too late to go. I sometimes figure I should have asked her to marry me except I figured she was way too pretty for me. She was pretty and all and we dated for some time but I sure am glad that I didn't ask her to marry me. It would be just my luck if she broke it off two weeks before the wedding. Somehow she just didn't fit like she was family. She never would have been happy with who I turned out to be. She wanted a white picket fence and I am not sure that would have fit for me.

Honey

Two marriages later and a lot of bumping from pillar to post I finally married my Honey. She's patient, smart and pretty. What more could I ask for? She grew up in a religious family. Ma liked that about her right off. She's as practical as Ma and loves popping into the Dollar Store to buy some kid or another a present. Honey is the reason that I live in the city. She loves the country but hates farming. She tolerates me having a pet rabbit but puts her foot down about a cat or a dog. She never grew up with any pets and isn't about to start now. "Feeding chickens and milkin' cows is honest noble work" she says, "but I'm getting my eggs and milk from A&P, thank you very much."

One thing that Honey loves is making apple crisp. She has never made it the same way twice but she always makes plenty to give away. She always takes apple crisp to the family reunion and there is never a speck left.

*   *   *

At our family reunions we mostly just get together and pitch horse shoes and talk over the barby. Ma always makes up giant burgers and Pa flips them. Every year Ma says "Pa, you just stay there an' flip 'm. Don't go off none or they'll burn." Every year Ma says the same thing and every year Pa says "Ma, I wish you wouldn't, I wish you wouldn't always tell me what I already know. I never burned 'm last year an' I ain't burned 'm ever an' I ain't gunna burn 'm this year." Then every year Ma says the exact same thing back "Pa, you burned 'm one year an that's all I know." As the screen door flaps behind her she yells one more time "Don't go wanderin' off none."

The family reunion wouldn't be the same if we didn't hear Ma and Pa grumble a bit. They love each other loads but I guess after sixty years of marriage they just got there own way about them and nothing's going to change.

Ma and Pa

Ma is a feisty old gal and gives Pa his no-for a couple of times a day. Ma is always trying to get Pa to take his nose out a his books. "Pa. Stop your readin' an take out the garbage. Put down your book an' get to the store for me."

Pa likes his reading an I don't even know if Ma can read. Pa must have near over three hundred books and I've never seen Ma read any of them. One day he'll give'm all to the lendin' library that's out front of the post office an' then they'll have near twice as many as they got now. Ma says "I'm just too busy with cleanin', cookin', an bakin' to give no bother to no books."

Ma is practical about everything and Pa lives in his head figuring this and figuring that. He figured out how to water all the pigs in one go with a hose and a trough an how to send straw down to the horses without breaking his back. Pa says "Just a little bit a lazy makes a man smart." Ma says "Yer too lazy an' yer books is only good for fire startin'." Pa says "Ya gotta understand yesterday to know tamara." Ma says "Put down yer cyclopedia and get me some firewood or I'll wack you with "A to C.""

The one thing that my Ma is not practical about is Christmas. Ma says, "Cleanin', cookin', an bakin' is what the dear baby Jesus would want me doin'. That and buying presents and going to church a few extra times I figure is what Christmas is all about." Ma is more generous and sometimes even more kind than Pa likes. She starts buying presents for just about everyone under the sun, on sale, in January, every year and keeps going ''before Christmas Eve. By the time December comes around all she has to worry about is getting Pa and me to cut the perfect tree and get it put up in the living room, in the corner, beside the piano; for Ma, the earlier the better.

Ma is not a particularly dispassionate person but on the other hand she was not very emotional. To this day I have never seen her cry not even on that one Christmas Eve back a few years. As usual us brothers and sisters were all over to Ma and Pa's big house for the ritual Christmas Eve family gathering. Just imagine the Walton's standing around the piano singing and you get the picture. Ma was standing proud in front of the grand tree wearing what she called her best Sunday goin' to church dress admiring the fine job that Pa and me had done pickin' and cuttin' the biggest tree we had ever had. "Pa, are you sure it's gunna fit safe in that bucket? Don't want it fallin' over or nothin' foolish like that."

"Ma, you are always worryin'. Just enjoy it quiet."

It was a fine tree indeed, all decked out with fine glass balls, popcorn strings and delicate ornaments that have been in the family for generations. Everyone of them had a special memory for Ma. "Put'm ginger, Put'm ginger" she would say as we gingerly put them, one by one, on the tree. Presents bulged from under the long bows looking just like last year's Christmas card.

Well, like I was saying, Ma was standing there admiring the tree holding two glasses of cranberry Christmas punch, one in each hand, while Pa went off to get his camera. Well just as sure as cats got whiskers, Ma's mouth dropped open. She became paralyzed and speechless, as the tree slowly teetered to the left, then slowly wobbled to the right. It tilted ever so slightly back and then in a split second with a lurch flung itself forward like it had a mind of its own and kept on coming. Ma was so mesmerized with shock that she couldn't move a muscle. In a last second flinch of desperation she jerked back and both glasses of red punch flew down the front of her finest. She stood there for what seemed like an eternity with Grams' glass angel shattered at her feet. With everyone stunned into quivering silence no one moved or said a word. With a stoic sense of calm, Ma handed the empty glasses to Pa and walked peacefully to her room. Pa was smart enough to get the tree put back up and never mentioned it ever again. He was smart that way.

Ma showed up a few minutes later in a different dress and asked Pa to get her a glass of punch. "Just one please an' ... only make it half." Ma sat down a safe distance from the tree and asked if anyone would like to sing "Oh Christmas Tree."

Christmas and Easter were very important commemorations in our house. Ma tried to instill in us the importance of the virgin birth and the resurrection. It wasn't "before I was almost sixteen that I realized not everyone celebrated the birth of Jesus let alone believed he was the son of God.

Ma and Pa lived in that farm house from what seems like the beginning of time. It used to be my Pa's Grampa's farm way back about a hundred and fifty years or more. Pa says the farm is mine if I want it when him and Ma are gone but I'm no farmer. Ma says I'm just a bit too lazy to make me smart. Pa used to say I just needed a girl and then I would want the farm. Ma used to say I need a kick in the pants, and Pa was too buried in his books to give it to me. I have been married to Honey now for five years and I still don't want the farm.

I grew up on the farm with my six brothers and sisters. Starting with the oldest it is Kimberley, Charlotte, Sarah and Mary, then me then Christopher. With my Pa I was the only other fellow on the farm when Chris packed up at about age sixteen, married an American girl, pretty gal. Can hardly blame him for wandering off and started work in a tire factory in Detroit. That's been over twenty years now and I have long stopped hoping my little brother would come back home where I can see more of him. Chris hasn't been to our family reunion in years.

Little Brother Chris

I was going to start by saying Chris was my favourite brother but being my only brother that goes without saying. Same goes for him being my most handsome brother and for that matter he's my smartest, tallest brother too, but everyone pretty much says the same things when they are talking about the two of us. On the farm Chris was my deepest dearest friend. I say "was" not 'cause he's dead or nothing like that but simply because ever since his wife stole him from me I hardly ever see him anymore. Chris, being my little brother, used to follow me everywhere I went. I'd go feed the pigs and there was little Chrisie. I'd go pick peas, for Ma, for supper and there was little Chrisie. Down to the mail box and there was Chrisie. Because we had a two holer on the farm, even when I went out to the out-house to be alone there was my little brother Chris sitting beside me. I say that he got to be so smart, handy, even tall and handsome, because he hung around me so much.

With Chris gone and before my sisters got married, it seemed that I lived with a bunch a girls for too many years. This might be the reason I was not in too much of a hurry to get married with so many women always around. There was Little Grams living only a couple a miles down the road and there was no man there and there was Big Grams living in the city and there was no man there. It seems to me that I had all the women in my life that I needed. Didn't know I needed a wife "before I fell in love with Honey.

*   *   *

I look forward to family reunions so I can see my sisters and all their kids. It seems there's a hole heap of them now. Ma keeps a calendar with everyone's names and birth dates just so she doesn't forget anybody. Ma is kind and thoughtful that way, always picking up something at the dollar store for someone.

Sister Kimberley

My big sister, Kimmy, is a lovely girl with three marriages under her belt, three skinny kids, two boys and a girl and no husband or boyfriend in sight. The oldest of all of us she always seems to be a bit of a lost soul eating away the distance of life, one delicious, cream- filled, Krispy Kream at a time.

She is, shall I say, a rather hefty gal. When she stomps into the room and flops onto the couch, springs sing and pillows puff; the place rocks and shakes like a combine or thresher drove into the room. You will have to pardon my exaggeration and perhaps unkind description of my darling sister; I love her dearly but when she is wearing her bright red, bulging, spandex shorts they scream under stress like a giant bowl of cherry jello poured into a pair of pantihose. God forbid those pantihose should ever get a run in them.

When Merve, her first husband disappeared, cousin Mike speculated, "She probably e't 'im." Mike stuck a chicken wing in his mouth and sucked the meat off the bone. "Just like that is how she would'a done it," he said with a grin as he flung the stripped bone clattering to his plate.

"Sis, How are yah? So glad that you and the kids could make it. A family reunion isn't the same without your giant salad. Put your bowl in the kitchen and say hi to Ma. She's somewhere in or out." I reach way over her enormous bosom to give her a peck on her pale white cheek. "Can I get'ya anything while I'm up. Piece a celery or something." We try our best to be encouraging by offering something other than chips and beer. Here at the family reunion it is no problem but at my place there's usually little else. Honey, sometimes I can't remember her real name, hates to cook and I hate to eat her cooking even more so more often than not we eat out at the Golden Gates restaurant just down the street. They have a TV and "all you can eat" chips on Tuesdays. Honey and me head there most evenings, have dinner and watch "Everyone Loves Raymond" and "Friends" reruns. I mostly tune out when Friends comes on but Honey loves them and would stay sipping gently on her one beer for hours if she could.

Sorry, but back to my dear sister Kimmy. She comes over to our house quite often just to get away from the kids. They are in high-school and playing sports in the evening but when they are home the music is turned up high as if they had socks in their ears. With their friends over it is more than poor Kimmy can stand.

Honey and I don't mind her coming over but I wish she would leave her little flea-bitten chi-wawa at home. Chee Chee, as Kimmy calls it, flinches in fear every time I come near. I have tried giving it dog biscuits and even bones from our rib dinners with Bill and Juli but still Chee Chee flinches and runs as soon as I get within neck wringing distance to the ugly mutt.

Kimmy eventually goes home when she figures her kids are in bed. She puts Chee Chee up on her bountiful chest and strolls home in those ugly floppy slippers that Little Grams gave her as a shower present for her third wedding. Flop-flop, flop-flop every step of the way as she takes her time in the cool August night. Stopping to look in the windows of the picture framing gallery she dreams of who she could have been if she had had the nerve to take those summer-school art lessons when she was just thirteen.

None of us had much of any encouragement to get an education let alone do something as frivolous as art. I too have often wondered just what I would be doing today if I had gone to college or, God forbid, to university.

Sisters Charlotte and Sarah

Like Kimmy, Charlotte and Sarah were sweet likable girls. One of them needed a bit a help in the brains department but I won't say who that is because she made up for it in the prettiness of her being a girl.

I grew up with the sweet smell of rose water lingering wherever they went. Charlotte and Sarah were far from being tomboys. They hated snakes and toads and stopped skinny dipping in Little Grams pond when they were just five or six. By the time I moved out from home and married Honey I was used to seeing frilly underpants hanging in the bathtub with piles of makeup on the counter. Wal-Mart's beauty counter obviously made a bunch off of them two.

On Sundays us men folk would give up waiting for our turn in the bathroom. Chris, Pa and me would use the outhouse and the hand pump outside the kitchen after we did our chores, before going to church.

Charlotte got married just before Christmas the year after Chris moved to Detroit. She wore a magical long flowing white dress that she borrowed from Auntie May and a flaming red cape that she borrowed, sight unseen, from a girlfriend. She didn't know it was bright red 'before it showed up the day of the wedding. Pa almost had a cow when he saw it and Ma was not pleased either but Charlotte just rolled with the fun of it and said "They might forget my weddin', they might forget my dress but nobody is going to forget my bright red cape." She flung the hood up over her parlour fancied hair and strutted out to Uncle Bill's new Buick and never thought anymore about it.

Sarah went to school in Toronto; the Distant Stink I call it. We never saw her much for about three years because it was so far away. When she finally graduated with honours she moved back home, got married within a year to the feed truck driver and started having babies one after the other 'before she had two miscarriages. The doctor said she had better stop at the even half dozen she already had. From being the prettiest to being the smartest in her class she ended up having the biggest hippo hips and was the best Ma you could ever imagine. Her and her family were always the life of the family reunion, every time, bringing enough fried chicken to feed a small army.

Sarah was the only one of us kids to get an education. It kinda bugs me that she threw it away on making babies but on the other hand I am happy she is happy. What more can we possibly ask for in life.

Sister Mary

Mary Beatrice was named after Aunt Mary Eddy, my pa's favourite great aunt. She was the tomboy of the four girls. For years some thought that she was a brother, always in overalls and a t-shirt, bare feet and a plaster on her elbow. Unlike her three sisters she liked snakes and toads and had an insect collection, three pet rabbits, two gerbils, crickets in a box with grass and a rooster that she called Charlie.

Mary's favourite thing was swimming in Little Grams pond. She didn't understand why Little Grams all of a sudden started to make her wear a t-shirt when she went swimming. Mary and I hung around like Chris and I used to before he moved away. We did almost everything together. Unlike with Chris though I was safe to be alone in the outhouse alone.

Mary was a rascal. She liked to play pranks on Pa. She was always changing the time on his alarm clock so that he'd get up too early or late for starting chores. One time when Ma was away at Kimmy's helping for a few days when Kimmy had her third baby she convinced Pa that it was Saturday when it was really Sunday. Nobody went to church that Sunday and Ma was real mad at Pa for not showing up. Ma said "You are one step closer to hell than heaven. The Lord Baby Jesus might forgive you but it'll take me some time."

The best, or was it the worst, trick that Mary played was to convince her teacher that Pa had died in a thrasher accident. She moped and cried for a week saying she just couldn't do her homework, on account that she was mournin' somethin' awful. Mary got in a heap of trouble when the teacher sent home flowers to Ma with a note of condolence.

Mary still lives at home with Ma and Pa. She said that she is never going to move. I figure that Mary should have the farm when Ma and Pa finally hitch their wagon that one last time.

Now that I'm telling you about all of the women folk in my life, I'd better tell you about my grams. Seems to me that I had a bunch of them. Two were my real grams, Little Grams as us kids used to call her and then there was Big Grams, and there was Nans, Granny and Mumzy. It wasn't till I was near grown up that I learned that I only had two real grandmothers: Big Grams and Little Grams. None of them will be at the family reunion as they are all gone now except for Mumzy but her not being family she wouldn't be coming anyway.

Little Grams

Little Grams was my pa's ma. She was a wiry, spunky little lady that kept us kids in place with a stern look that we called, Grams' "evil eye". If giving us the evil eye didn't work she'd raise the yard stick or wooden spoon high in the air at us. That's all it ever took. We'd know better than to rile her any more. We'd smarten up and head out to the barn or down to the pond where we couldn't give her any trouble.

Little Grams hired me to clean her windows and cut the grass at her farm. I kept some spending money in my pocket when I was growing up. I used to hop on my bike, a blg blue one with chrome butterfly handle bars. I'd whip down the dusty country road to Little Grams' house. Her old mutt, Spunky, would see me coming, tare full tilt over the cedar rail fence, down the lane and across the hay field, just to get to me as I arrived to the rusty old mail box. Spunky would jump up onto my lap, into my handle bar carry box and wag his tail in my face as I set up the narrow lane to Grams' white frame house. I used to hang out at Little Grams for most of my summer, not even go home some nights. I'd pitch a tent that I made out of old burlap feed bags, sling it over the clothes line and fall asleep listening to the summer breeze in the trees. Spunky, would curl up beside me an whistle as he snored. Those were the best summer days of my life. Sometimes I long for such simplicity.

Big Grams

Big Grams was my ma's ma. It wasn't that she was so big but it was simply that she was bigger than Little Grams.

Big Grams was my favourite, at least when I was there that is. She was the city Grams. She didn't have the vast country fields of emerald green for me to get lost in; she didn't have a crystal clear duck pond, horses or a dog but she did treat me like I was a prince. Big Grams saved baking day for when I came over. She would measure and I'd mix. Her oatmeal cookies with raisins were the best I'd ever have. Licking the spoon and spatula was the best part of baking but being with Grams and her gentle nature was what made me come back almost once a week. When I got a bit older, Ma and Pa trusted me to ride my bike into the city all on my own and stay the night. Big Grams trusted me with going to the store to pick up some groceries, usually some special treat that she knew I'd fancy.

One night when I was just little, my sister, Kimmy and I stayed the night at Big Grams' house. Right in the middle of the night I quietly reached over and shook my sister, "Sis, Sis … there's a bear in Grams' room. We have to shoo it or it'll eat 'er. Sis, wake up." My sister, blurry eyed, turned over and muttered, "That's no bear, that's grammy snorin', now go back to sleep." With fear still quaking deep in my chest I pulled the rough wool blanket to my chin and prayed like I never prayed before. "Dear Father-Mother God, don't let that bear eat Grams and if you do, please God, don't let him eat me too!"

Nans, Granny and Mumzy

As I said, I had three other grams in my life that I also thought were my real grandmothers. They were, Nans, Granny and Mumzy. Nans was a great, great aunt. I figured she was near 110. I think she must have died and no one bothered to tell me. It was only in hindsight that I realize I hadn't seen her for years. Ma later told me that she just never woke up one morning. I was a might disturbed by that idea. "How are you supposed to know if you are dead if you just don't wake up," I asked? Ma just looked at me cross the same as when she caught me looking at girls underpants in the

Sears' catalogue one time. I told her that I was lookin' for the bicycle section but she never believed me.

Granny was a special person in my life but she wasn't my real grandmother. She was just this nice little old lady that lived down the road. She seemed to be everyone's granny. Turns out her name was Mrs. Clark. Us kids liked to go over to her house to see her pet skunk. It was de-skunked so it was more like a cat and yup, it's name was Daisy.

Granny used to give us cookies and milk every time we went over. One day when I was coming home from school, there was a moving truck outside her house emptying the place. They said she moved to an old folks home but I figured they murdered her 'cuz they wanted all of her stuff. All I know for sure is that I never saw her or Daisy again.

Mumzy was my fifth grandmother. She used to read us kid's stories on her front porch and let us feed her cats little cat cookies. She had a grey moustache that would put a walrus to shame. It would prick your cheek when she bent down to give you a kiss. It was a small price to pay for the peek down her blouse to her pale voluptuous womanhood. Mumzy is still around but she moves a lot slower these days and she still has lots of cats.

With all of these grandmother figures in my life I didn't once stop to wonder where the men were. Turns out one was chased off by Little Grams because he was bootlegging rum down to the U.S. of A. back in prohibition times and one was killed in the Great WW. Big Grams never stopped ranting "I lost your grandpa in a war to re-divide the colonies and make rich men richer. No King of England never asked me if I wanted to pay the price of my young husband."Big Grams never got married again and was sore at the King for the rest of her life.

Another one packed up and took off with Bethy, the town floozy. Bethy was the prettiest woman I had ever seen. Bright red lips, deep blue eyes and a set of cantaloupes that just about knocked you out. Uncle Eric told my pa, "I give Bethy a ride in my Caddy one time before it was full a rust. Oh man, Aunt Mary was mighty mad and give him a black eye to make me think better the next time." Uncle Eric leaned over closer to my pa, "The black eye was worth it, wink wink, if you know what I mean."

* * *

Every year you can count on most of the aunts and uncles showing up to the family reunions. My Pa had eight brothers and sisters and my Ma had eight so it made for a heap a aunts, uncles and cousins. Still to this day I can't keep them all straight. Sometimes I figure we should have name tags at our family reunions. Last year my little niece, Cookie, as I call 'er (I'm the only one that is allowed to call her that.) leaned over to me and whispered, "Who is that guy in the purple Hawaiian shirt with the hairy white legs?" Turned out it was my Uncle Bill who she hadn't seen for years.

Uncle Bill

Good old Uncle Bill is usually recovering from one surgery or another and hasn't been to a family reunion since I can't remember. Aunt Kate, his young, and I mean young and very pretty, kinda short, wife always comes by herself and always brings pictures of Uncle Bill's latest surgery along with her best deviled eggs. Cookie said "Them deviled eggs is worth die'n' for an' the pictures of the surgery wanna make you die."

Cousin Mike speculates every time he sees her, "Katie is a young tart and nothing but a gold digger, she's only after Willie's money. One day Willie ain't gunna survive one of those surgeries and that'll be the last time that we ever see her at one of our family does." Pa always pipes up in Auntie Kate's defense, "There is one thing wrong with your surmise Mike, Willie ain't got no money you silly dope. He lost his second last dime on that Cup-O-Matic hot cup a soup car plug in contraption years ago. Don't you remember him tryin' to convince you to run some wires and hoses over your engine so as you could have hot soup at the press of a button while you drove. That's why you still get soup packets every year for Christmas."

Uncle Bill is a farmer like most of us, but he now sells AmWay on the side. He used to bring his catalogues and samples to family reunions until a year ago Aunt Kate whacked him in the arm and hollered, "Why do you need remindin' you old fart, you have been trying to sell dish detergent and stain remover to your cheap family for years and no one has ever bought any." I didn't want to remind her that ma bought a bottle of dish detergent just because she felt sorry for him one year. She put the bottle under the sink and told him every time he got out his catalogues, "It ain't finished Willy, I'll tell you when I need more." She told him this, year after year and refused to use a drop of it. What ma doesn't know is that pa used it up along time ago to kill tomato bugs and filled the bottle with water so ma wouldn't know.

One time Uncle Bill gave a demonstration of how good his detergent worked. To show how environmentally safe it was he said he would drink some to prove it was harmless. Everyone perked up and egged him on. The demonstration kit said to mix a certain part detergent with a certain part water. He got the parts mixed up and spent the rest of that family party in the outhouse. To this day if anyone is the least bit "irregular" , if I can be so bold as to use that word, they ask Uncle Bill if he has any of his "Willy's Wonder Drug" with him.

We have a lot of aunts and uncles that come to the family reunion. We have some great aunts, no great uncles left, plus some older second cousins that we call auntie and uncle and a few friends of the family that we call auntie and uncle as well. It's no wonder I can't keep them all straight. One more invented aunt or uncle will turn our family tree into a tangled crooked bush. I swear one year I'm gonna bring name tags to keep everyone straight.

One of the aunts and uncles that always come is Uncle Al and Aunt Allison. Everyone mostly calls them Al and Al. They always come and every year they bring a huge carrot cake, so big that they have to put it on their ironing board in the back of the pickup just to get it here. I have to remember to ask Pa which branch of the family shrub Uncle Al sprung up from.

Uncle Al

My Uncle Al is a smoker and proud of it. "Smoked since I was ten," he bragged. He swears he loves it. "I'll smoke till the day I die." A stiff, lumpy, hand-rolled fag droops from his nicotine-stained lip, bobbing as he talks, always squinting in his right eye from the drifting smoke. He rambles on and on as he always does seemingly without a breath; squinting, talking, bobbing.

He could talk your ear off about anything or nothing. He once told me a story about a horse with no teeth and a stubby tail. He jabbered on and on about this silly horse that had only one shoe until his rollie was nothing but an unflicked ash that eventually dropped onto his stained Molson Golden t-shirt that he almost always wore.

Don't know what Uncle Al does for a living, maybe nothing, maybe that's why he smoked rollies and is as skinny as a rail.

Little Grams called him Aloysius one day when she caught him swiping a cigarette from her purse. Pinching this or that was hardly a surprise to anyone but no one knew his real name was Aloysius Sheldon Marvin until Grams blurted it out. No wonder he kept his real name secret.

In one of cousin Mike's speculative moods, which seems to be most of the time, he said, "Did you know that Uncle Al was in jail one time when we all thought that he was livin' out west workin' on the Athabasca oil rigs? What he was in for nobody knows. He must'a stole somethin' from someone and got pinched for it. You can see it in his eyes can't ya? They are just too beady or close together or something. His eye brows are too thick and meet in the middle, you can see it in his face."

Aunt Allison

Uncle Al was married to Aunt Allison. Everyone called her Auntie but the fact is she wasn't any one's aunt 'cause Al and Allison never got married. They lived in sin, as some called it, and even then they only lived together some of the times. No one really understood why she would disappear for months at a time. She seemed a bit weird to me, sometimes more than others.

Cousin Mike constantly threw out his speculations – "I bet she's is in jail," he said one time. "I tried to sell her a life insurance policy one time and all she said was, she figured she didn't have no rights to live and walked away from me standin' holdin' her limp paper plate full of tater salad." Some times she was a gem and sometimes she was... well I will just say... not.

My pa said she was an enigma. I was puzzled over that word for months. For the longest time I thought he said she was a magnum but that didn't seem to make any sense neither. My pa always did know too many big words. He was always kind to Aunt Allison. He figured that everyone should be treated right. He gave her his chair once when she was pregnant with little cousin Vicky. Haven't seen her for a while, come to think of it.

Auntie Pat

Auntie Pat is an Irish gal with red hair and lots of freckles, is pleasant in the personality department and mighty generous when it comes to bringing food to the family reunions. Fried chicken, enough for everyone, macaroni salad 'cause its Pa's favourite with lots a dill pickle chopped in. She always brings dozens of white buns fresh from the grocery store. She says, "None of those cheap homemade kind. I like the fresh white ones from A&P."

Everything she makes is mighty good except for the mustard pickles. Ma, one time said, "Patzi has nice freckles." Patzi thought she said nice pickles, an from then on Auntie Pat takes her pickles everywhere she goes. Everybody hates them but because everyone is so darn afraid of hurting her feelings they always say "Mighty fine pickles Patzi, as good as usual?" She always leaves the open jar instead a taken them home. Pa discovered that they make a mighty good plaster for bringing down the swelling on the horses ankles if they get twisted in a gopher hole. The only problem with this fine remedy is that it attracts too many flies.

Uncle Eugene keeps telling the story over and over again about when they were coming to a family reunion one year. Patzi promised Ma that she would buy a pie fresh from the grocery store on the way over. She knows that Ma loves cherry pies an got all torn up inside when she mulled over buying her own favourite strawberry pie or cherry pie for Ma. Patzi's generosity must have been at an all time low that day 'cause she bought the strawberry pie and said Ma would never know she had a choice. Funny thing is that when Patzi opened the box and presented the pie it was cherry. Ma thanked and thanked Patzi for being so thoughtful for remembering her favorite.

Patzi never tried to cheat the Saint of Generosity ever again. "The angels switched the pies before I got there for dinner," she used to say and she never bought a strawberry pie for herself ever again. "It was divine intervention." Patzi said over and over again.

Uncle Eric

No family reunion would be the same without Uncle Eric. Uncle Eric is my Pa's older brother. He should have been the one to get my Pa's farm after Gramps died but Uncle Eric always said, "I'll have nothin' to do with no farmin'. Feedin' a bunch of dumb animals at one end and shovelin' manure at the other end, every day, twice a day, day in and day out, month after month, year after year is the life of a sorry man." He let you know it whenever he saw dirt under your finger nails or manure stuck to your heels.

Now there is one of those enigmas if I ever saw one. He was rich or thought he fooled us into thinking he was rich. He drove a sky blue 68 Mercedes-Benz full of rust. Said it was a classic and refused to get rid of her. I figured the binder twine that kept the trunk closed was the only classic thing about the car. "Classic poverty." said cousin Mike, under his breath, every time he saw the blue smoke belch from the broken tail pipe.

Uncle Eric was my funny uncle. Every year he always had a story with a funny twist. One year he told a story about his parrot called Crackers. Turned out he had a dog that liked to eat crackers, liked to eat anything for that matter. Another year he told a story about when he was a pilot in Word War II but turned out the only thing he flew was the gas truck back and forth from plane to plane.

Fine story teller though. Didn't matter if they were true. As long as we would keep the fire going in the fire pit out back he would keep spinin' yarn. Everyone was always ready for another story. No one kept track of the details to catch him on the truth. The fact is the truth didn't matter none to no one.

One year when I was just ten or so while everyone else was pitchin' horseshoes or gettin' dinner ready I asked him about a big black feather with a white tip that he had stuck in the dash of his blue Mercedes-Benz. He told me with great conviction that my pa was BBQing some big thick steaks when an eagle came swoopin' down and snatched the steaks right from off the sizzlin' grill. Just as that giant bird sunk his claw size talons into those steaks my pa grabbed the bird's legs with all his might and was dragged over the hot coals into the air. My pa didn't buy big fat steaks very often so he was not about to let go. As that eagle flapped with my pa danglin' he reached up with all his might and plucked that feather right out of that eagle's bum. The eagle squawked like he had been shot in the head and without thinking let go of the steaks along with my pa. Well, luck would have it that my pa fell into the lake and wasn't hurt none. With the feather and steaks clenched between his teeth he swum to shore, plopped the steaks back on the still hot grill and gave the feather to his big brother, my Uncle Eric. Wasn't till I was near 16 that I figured out that eagles don't like cooked meat and wouldn't a swooped down for no hot cookin' steaks any how.

One thing that is amazing about our family reunions is all the story tellin' that goes on and it isn't just Uncle Eric that spins a good yarn. Uncle Girwood can keep even Uncle Eric tilted forward in his chair.

Uncle Girwood

Uncle Girwood looks to me like he is about 110. He is the second cousin, twice removed of my Aunt Kate's first husband's brother's oldest son. He isn't even on the family tree but an uncle, nonetheless. He must not have any of his own family because he keeps coming to our family reunions and we welcome him with open arms.

Ma said he won't eat anything but grilled cheese sandwiches and french fries; don't know what he would have for breakfast but judging by the front of his stained shirt he always uses catsup with his fries. I did see him eating watermelon one time but I think he only ate that because he wanted to spit watermelon pips off the deck with the kids.

Uncle Girwood is as much of a story teller as anyone I know. With a grilled cheese sandwich clenched in one hand, he would light into a story like he was havin' it for lunch. He didn't just tell a story because it happened or 'cause it was true, because it was funny or sad, he told a story because it would make you think.

My favourite was the one about the chickens boxed up on a truck going to the slaughterhouse. I heard the story many times before but I always like how he would get you going. First he would get you thinking about freedom and making the right choices in life. Then he would start in by telling about this one chicken named Wilbur.

There was nothing particular special about Wilbur. He was just a normal, average, run-a-the-mill chicken. The only thing is that he took advantage of being in the right place at the right time. You might say he was smart enough to see an opportunity and brave enough to take advantage of it. It all started by accident when Wilbur stuck his wing out a small hole in the crate. He wiggled around a bit flappin' it in the breeze as the truck rumbled down the dusty gravel road. After a minute of flappin' his wing he realized he could squeeze his head out. The wind in his face was wonderful. Feathers were flutterin' in the wind of the fast truck like he had never felt before and it felt marvelous.

For the first time in his life he could taste freedom and he wanted more. Wilbur first felt just a bit silly with his wing and head stuck out a the crate. Can you imagine? All of the other chickens were looking at him strange, squawking at him, telling him they ain't gunna help him if he gets stuck good and can't move none. Wilbur ignored all of the cackling from his friends. With a bit more squirmin' and wrigglin'

Wilbur manages to get another wing out of the crate, then half of his body, then all of a sudden with a mighty squeeze he was outside of the crate holdin' on for dear life flappin' in the wind wishin' he was back in the safety of his crate. "Oh my gosh," thought Wilbur. "What on earth have I done?"

As time went on he got used to the feeling of the rushing air that he had never felt before. Wilbur didn't feel afraid no more and felt better than he had ever felt. He starts squawkin' at his chicken friends. "I is free, I is free and you silly saps is still stuck in your crates. Come on you guys, with just a bit of a squeeze you can come out and join me." One of his brother chickens stuck out his wing and then his head and feels the rush of the wind. Wilbur sees him trying to make it to freedom and spurs him on. "Everyone can be free If you just try."

Wilbur takes a look at the open fields that are rushing by, he squats down and gets ready to take a jump off the truck. "Come on guys, lets go for it." With those last few words still clinging to his beak he takes a flying leap off the truck towards the open fields. In mid air as he turns to wave to his buddy chickens he gets splottowed by an on-coming truck. The air is instantly filled with feathers. Chicken parts is mashed on the truck windshield. Wilbur had no idea what hit him. His chicken buddies squawked in horror, quickly pulling in their heads, tucking in their wings and shrunk into silence. "Poor Wilbur," one clucked. "He would still be alive if he hadn't been so impulsive as to try to be free." Just then, with no one noticing, the truck rumbled to a gentle stop outside the slaughterhouse gate.

I have heard this Wilbur story over and over again, year after year. It never stopped making me think. Now I look around our family and wonder just which one of us is Wilbur. Which one of us was just about to get out of the crate?

Our family is as modelin' a bunch of odd balls as you would see at any family reunion. We aren't your normal family by any stretch. None of us ever had any special jobs and none of us, including me, ever got any real schoolin' side from cousin Bill but don't let that name confuse you none just 'cause we have five Bills in our family. Two cousin Bills, a brother-in-law Bill, handsome devil of a guy and two uncle Bills. The only one that is half ways to smart is cousin Bill the professor. Him and his wife come almost every year exceptin' when he is invited to present a lecture at some fancy smancy university in some exotic place like Hawaii. I figure he managed to get out of the crate if no one else has.

Cousin Bill and Cousin Bill

Dr. Billy Boy is what I call him. He is a doctor of clouds and rain an' stuff like that. He's always talking about the green house effect, global warming and other science stuff like that. He goes way up north and does tests on the ice checking out how the polar bears are doing. Nice guy but only had two white shirts and two pair a grey flannel pants to his name. It wasn't 'before his honeymoon when his new wife got a hold of him and wised him up to the fact that he looked a might peculiar on the beach with a grey neck tie and black shoes. I figured that most of his body had never seen the light of day 'before the new wife put him in a golf shirt from Sears, a fancy pair a shorts and a pair of them open-toed sandals that you see Italians wearing. Now he passes himself off as almost normal when you see him at a family do.

At least he never shows up with mud on his heels like my other cousin Bill. Willy, as we mostly call him, usually comes to family gatherings straight off the farm and smellin' like it too. He lives out in the sticks way up the road from Little Grams with his big black dog, Rex. He said he feeds Rex gun powder to keep 'im mean so as to keep strangers and foxes away from the old barn. "Poor ol' thing." Ma would say, "He never knew no lovin' from no one since he was a pup. Willy kicks 'im and jabs 'im as he passes just 'cause he is an ornery kinda guy 'im self. I reckon that Willy wouldn't know how to love nothin' or nobody."

Uncle Eric said he was going to pay Bethy to go out an give him some lovin' that he has missed out on since his Ma died when he were just 10. Willy's Pa died when Willy was just 12, left his heart broke and he stayed on the farm ever since. Uncle Al and my Pa used to go over regular to make sure he was ok. They felt mighty bad for him but there was no way that they or no one could get him to leave his Pa's farm and move in with them.

Uncle Eric perked up noticing the cloud of dust streamin' up the lane. "Someone else is arriving. Looks like Willy's pickup. Crappers, it looks like he's got a woman with 'im!" Everyone turned and gawked with chins dropped as Willy got out of his truck and came strolling over with his hair shinin' and slicked back like it was dabbed with bacon grease. In one arm he was carryin' a watermelon, on the other arm he was clung to by a pretty, but shy-looking gal, with long brown hair. Her pretty, pale blue dress fluttered in the breeze as she walked pressed beside Willy. Willy didn't say anything, he just grinned from ear to ear like the time he won the hog callin' contest a few years back. Uncle Mike hollers "You old goat. We ain't seen you for so long that we figured you was in jail. Woo Eee, who's the pretty gal! How much did you have to pay 'er to come with you?" Susie, Mike's wife, punches him in the arm hard as she could and told him, "Shut up you knuckle head and be good."

Everyone gathered around Willy and his new gal. Ma reached over and took the watermelon from him and give him a kiss on his freshly shaved cheek. It has been a long time since anyone has seen him shaved and dapper. "Who's your gal Willy?" Ma asks, squeezing her hand in a welcoming way.

Mark the Mulch Man

I'm not just sure how our cousin, Mark the Mulch Man, as he is known to be called, fits into the family tree but we see him regularly at family reunions. For short we call him Mulch. If for some reason he doesn't come he always sends a fancy doggerel poem; he's the only real good writer in the family. If you haven't guessed he's big into mulching just about everything that decomposes.

I figure that Mulch is probably one of the very last hippies. He wears those Birkenstock open toed sandals, is kind of plump with long grey hair and a beard that comes down to the middle of his belly. He wears a dirty old t-shirt that says "Compost It" on the front. Cousin Mike figures it looks like it got lost in the compost for a while on account of it being so dirty.

Mulch is the environmentally friendly one in the family. He built a whole series of mulching bins like no one has ever seen. He built a wind mill out of old oil drums (I've never seen it spin even once), a solar panel out of tin cans and an old window and get this, an indoor compost toilet. Well who would have ever thought you would have an outhouse IN the house. The "piece of resistance" – pardon my French – is that he built a house out of bales of straw and stitched it together with binder twine. We still tease him that the big bad wolf is just around the corner and ready to blow his house down.

Every year Mulch shows up to the family reunion with a tofu cheese cake and muffins that end up in our compost.

*   *   *

A family reunion is a wonderful time for meeting up with folks you haven't seen for some time. It is an especially good time for seeing the kids running and having fun.

Two of Charlotte's kids come screaming around the corner soaked to the skin, with squirt guns blazing. Chee Chee is dripping wet and in hot pursuit. All attention vanishes from Willy and his new gal as Uncle Eric yells for them not to get him wet as Chee Chee darts between his legs. "Go give Uncle Fred a squirt an wake 'im up. It's probably time someone took 'im to the outhouse anyway."

Uncle Fred

I am sure that everyone in the world has an Uncle Fred. Our Uncle Fred, or Freddy, as everyone calls him, no one called him Frederic which was his real name, is a Bible thumpin' Baptist with a thick fake British accent.

When he was young he was tall, as skinny as a drink a water and as fast as a rabbit. Story has it that he was a message runner in the Great war running from one military operation to another with dispatches. He was brave as all get out, with lots of medals to prove it.

Freddy's in a wheelchair now and losing his marbles. He must be near 110 I reckon, half blind in one eye an can't hardly see out of the other, but every morning he gets up and pins his war medals onto his greying undershirt and sits beside the flag pole out front of his old-age home. Most of the time he sits and sleeps in the sun unless someone takes to talking to him in which case he pops to life and tells you one of his war stories.

He told me he served under General Eisenhower and General Grant when he fought the Boers at "Custard's" last stand. 'Cause I didn't have no real schooling like Bill I was just flabbergasted with amazement every time he told me a story. Like with Uncle Eric's stories it didn't matter if his stories were true or not. Just sitting with the old fart was enough to make the time pass for him and me.

* * *

The backyard all of a sudden seemed full of family and friendly faces. Four generations all standing around jawin'.   What a marvelous sight. Ma has come out to the back patio a few times and reminded Pa to get back to the BBQ and stay there else the burgers 'll burn.
"I w i i i s h y o u w o u l d n 't" Pa mutters as he waves to Ma like she was a fly hovering over the uncooked burgers. "The burgers is fine Ma, stop yer fussing and get Eric a ginger-beer before he heads home with his jello salad." Pa inches back towards Uncle Eric and defiantly turns his back to the now smoking BBQ. A couple of minutes go by an Uncle Eric pokes Pa and reminds him that he's neglecting his duty. "Ma will skin me if I burn any of those burgers," Pa says as he dashes back like a neglectful sentry. He flips open the lid and tosses a couple of charred burgers to Chee Chee. Any of the conspicuous pieces that Chee Chee wouldn't eat he stuffs down through the grate into the fire just in time as Ma returns with a ginger-beer for Uncle Eric. "Pa you is doing a fine job as usual." Ma pats Pa on the back and, as she heads back to the kitchen, she

looks over her shoulder, leans gently to Uncle Eric and says. "You keep 'im flipping Eric or I'll be blamin' you if he burns any." Ma shuffles off yelling behind her that she'll be back in a minute. "Don't go off none" she yells as the aluminum screen door hisses to a slow shut behind her.

Just as Ma is out a sight, Eugene, Pa's little brother, comes trundling around the corner carrying a big cooler with yet another watermelon perched on top. "Come and see my new car." Eugene yelps to Uncle Eric and Pa. With only a flinch of hesitation they both head off out of sight round front with most of the men folk trotting right behind 'm.

Uncle Eugene

Uncle Eugene, Gene, as most of us call him is a hefty, tall, handsome, man about twenty years younger than Pa, six three with a few extra pounds around the middle and still a full head of hair and a greying goatee. Auntie Pat, his wife, is always trying to get Uncle Eugene to eat salads instead of burgers and chips, beer and pizza, cookies and cake.

Uncle Eugene loves showing up every other year with a new car to show off to everyone. "She's a beaut" yelps Pa as he kicks the tires. "What year is she, how many kilometers she got on her? Not much rust and no dints, mighty sweet looking set a wheels, Gene. Let's take 'er for a spin." Before Pa can crawl in over the plush blue velvetine seats Gene starts on about how he dickered with the salesman and got 'im down a pretty penny, plus a full tank a gas.

Uncle Eugene was known for his powers of dickerin'. For Kimmy's wedding he was in charge of gettin' a hole mess a pop for the dance at the hall in Ancaster. He showed up with 110 bottles of pop that he simply paid the normal sale price for but boasted that he got the store to throw in a free watermelon. He has been teased about his powers of dickering ever since.

Picture this, Uncle Eugene's car is now filled to the brim with six laughing men carryin' on like they had never seen a used car before. Uncle Eugene hollers to Pa "You are a smart fella, what do you think I paid for her?" As they pull away over the gravel driveway, a sudden look of terror pales over Pa's face. He opens the door of the still-moving car and yells "Stop this bucket a bolts, I gotta get out!" He bolts out like a fourteen year old, tripping over his own feet as he tears toward the house without a word. With the gloom of fear gripped in his teeth, he dashes past the horseshoe pit and hurdles the sandbox in one stride. With a blur, he darts past the picnic table where Chee Chee is slobbering down a plate of salad that someone unstrategically left on the seat of their chair. Chee Chee flinches with guilt as Pa, with Olympian speed, turns the corner of the garage to see billows of smoke lapping up the vinyl siding, heaving like Indian smoke signals over the eaves into the clear blue sky.

With shrieks of terror, he pushes past Auntie Pat, bumping her slice of watermelon to the fresh-cut grass. Out of breath and heaving he comes face to face with the steely glare of Ma. She is standing there with a garden hose streaming water onto leaping flames. Pa, with the shrinking posture of a little boy quivers with his hands at his side as if he were standing in front of the school principal, can utter no words. With an almost smirk on her face, Ma turns to Pa and says in a calm but sarcastic voice, "Pa, stay at the BBQ an' don't wonder off none." With these words still forming in Pa's brain she turns the hose from the now steaming coals onto Pa who gasps for a breath without saying a word. Ma turns off the water and hands him the hose. In a calm voice Ma says, "Anyone want deviled eggs? They's Katie's best ever."

Pa stands there drenched from top to bottom with the drippin' hose dangling from his hand. Uncle Eric pokes Pa and says "Think you had better give that barby another squirt Bro? She's still kinda burning." Pa flinches into shivering consciousness and turns the hose back on the still hissing flames. "For a smart fella, I sure am stupid sometimes," Pa says as he kicks the picnic table. Chee Chee jumps with a yelp and scampers off. In the background Ma is heard saying to Auntie Pat "You seen my plate a salad? I put it down on my chair a minute ago when I came outside."

*   *   *

By now there must be near 15 cars and pickups lining the lane in the shade of the old oaks that run from the house to the mailbox. People are laughing and talking in little groups all over the place. The sun is shining, kids are running and swinging. The dogs are yelping and everyone is having a fine old time.

"Pa, here's more burgers for the barby. There's still more people arrivin' so I hope you can get that soggy thing lit again. Don't go walking off none."

Epilogue

The Drive Home

The sad part of every family reunion comes in the leaving. All the burgers and salads have been eaten, all of the paper plates have been picked up and burned in the bonfire, many licked clean by Chee Chee. All of the plastic cutlery and plastic glasses have been washed, dried and put away for next time. "Don't throw away none of them good plastics." Ma would remind us every year.

It seems like a heavy-hearted time, just Honey and me, starting the drive home back to the city and our little house. In the dark, now quiet, backyard hangs the double swing set, motionless. The big black rock has been put back on top of the garbage can. "Makes it 'coon proof" Pa would say. The crushed grass from all of the parked cars and pickups will linger as a sad reverie for a few days; lit by our headlights we turn to drive down the dark lane to the quiet, deserted country road.

Honey and I lament that even though we might see some of our family, perhaps as soon as the next day, it will not be before Christmas or longer that we would see the rest. There are no weddings planned for the near future and God forbid we get together again for another funeral anytime soon.

"Honey, you figure Pa turned off the gas on the barby?" I guess Ma would never forget such a detail. No matter how many times she might ask Pa, she'll have to get outa bed and check for herself. Hidden back in the recesses of Ma's memories there will always be that one time that two wieners and a half dozen chicken wings were found charred black and toasty warm the next morning. There will always be one mistake or another that Pa will never live down.

"I had a fine time as usual. What about you Honey? I think we had six watermelons this year. They must have been on sale at IGA. I might not have to eat for a week considering all the burgers and salad I had. Sure would have been nice if brother Chris could a come. I miss him. The price of gas makes it hard for him to take time off work and come all the way from Detroit. He promised Christmas though. I made him promise. I'll phone him in the morning and tell him what a fine time we all had and that everyone was asking after him.

Sure was nice that so many asked about Bear and said that they were sad that he passed on. We were all pretty thick with him. I remember the time he shot me with a BB rifle. He said that it was actually me that shot him. We argued and teased about that for years. I still miss him a lot. Him and Myrna. Such a shame they aren't with us anymore."

There is a long, quiet pause as the pickup truck hums south along #6 Highway towards the city. Driving in the dark is one of my favorite times to just be quiet and think. Honey and I hardly even need to say anything most of the ride home, but on the other hand it's a great time to spill the beans on something that has been turning over in the mind.

"Honey. I've been mulling something over for some time now. What do you think about me going back to school in the fall? I don't know for what and it's kinda late to be thinking about it now but somehow I feel it's time I moved forward. I'm feeling a bit stuck in the mud lately. I don't want to drive the milk truck for the dairy for ever and I don't want to be the chicken with his head and wing only part way out of the crate. That's all our family ever knows. Truckin' and farmin'. I just feel I'm a bit stuck in the mud lately."

The END

Biographical sketch of the author:

Richard Grove is known as the man of the 7 Ps – Poet, Potter, President, Photographer, Painter, Publisher, Public Speaker and sometimes person.

Richard was born into an artist family in Hamilton, Ontario, on October 7, 1953. With both parents artists and gallery owners he had a unique and early introduction into the world of visual art. His first experience with art was with photography when at the age of thirteen he purchased, with his father's enthusiasm and help, his first single lens reflex camera. Over the ensuing years, after leaving high school, he studied pottery at Mohawk College, design and pottery at Sheridan College, leading to his graduating in 1984 from the Experimental Arts Department at Ontario College of Art. In 1994 he graduated with honours from the Humber College, Arts Administration diploma course. In 2002 he returned to school to study computer courses relating to publishing.

Since graduating from Ontario College of Art, Richard has exhibited in more than twenty, solo and group exhibitions in Hamilton, Toronto, Boston, Calgary and

Grand Prairie. He has his art in over thirty corporate collections across Canada, the most prominent of which are Esso Resources, Continental Insurance, Alberta Energy Corporation and Calgary District Hospital Group. These four companies alone represent a collection of almost thirty pieces of his work. Among the many corporate collections are six commissions of different styles and mediums ranging from pastel on paper to acrylic on canvas.

Author reading at Purdy Fest in Marmora, Ontario, 2006

His photography and digital paintings have been on the cover of numerous books and periodicals. His book of digital paintings and poetry entitled "Sky Over Presqu'ile" was published in 2003, "Substantiality" a book of digital paintings was published in 2006 with a book of photography entitled "Oxido Rojo" released in the fall of 2006 followed by, in the same year, a book of photography entitled "terra firma".

Along with his visual art, Richard has been writing poetry seriously for decades and has had over 100 of his poems published in periodicals and has been published in over 30 anthologies from around the world. Including his poetry and photography he has 14 titles to his name. To mention only two of his poetry titles, his book entitled "Beyond Fear and Anger" was released in 1997 and his book published by Micro Prose, entitled "Poems For Jack" was released in 2002. He is also the author of numerous books with metaphysical themes including "The Mind–Body Connection", "Metaphysical Healing For a Secular Age" and "A Spiritual Study of Body". You can reach him at writers@hiddenbrookpress.com.

He is an editor and publisher and runs a growing publishing company Hidden Brook Press from which he publishes poetry contest anthologies and books of every genre for authors around the world. Aside from being a published poet, Richard has also exhibited his poetry in acrylic on paper paintings as well as in audio sculptures. For his poetry and prose, Richard has won a few small prizes and honourable mentions as well as a finalist spot in two contest anthologies. For his short stories he has won a top ten prize.

Richard is the founder of the Canadian Poet Registry, an archival information website that lists Canadian poets including: biographical information, their book titles and awards. One can view this website at - http://www.hidden brook press.com/Registry.htm. He was an active member of the Canadian Poetry Association for ten years serving on the executive for seven years including five as

President. He is the founding president of both the CCLA (2004) – Canada Cuba Literary Alliance - www.CanadaCubaLiterarAlliance.org and the CCLA Federation of Photographers (2006).

The CCLA has an international membership and boasts a full-colour literary journal called The Ambassador and a literary e-newsletter called The Envoy. He is the founding president of the Brighton Arts Council and the co-founder of the Purdy Country Literary Festival.

Richard has also been a public speaker MCing poetry readings and other literary events. He has been invited by a number of literary groups as Feature Speaker on various topics in Cuba, Germany, USA, New Zealand and Canada. He was also the Feature Author as publisher/poet in the October 1998 issue of "The Treasure Chest" published out of Virginia, USA and Feature Poet in "Poetry Canada" in 2004.

Richard now lives with his wife, also a writer, Kim, in Presqu'ile Provincial Park situated halfway between Toronto and Kingston, south of the 401 hwy. Their location is a constant inspiration for their work.

Books in the North Shore Series

Find full information at
– http://www.HiddenBrookPress.com/b-NShore.html

First set of five books

— **M.E. Csamer** – Kingston – "A Month Without Snow"
   – Prose – ISBN – 978-1-897475-87-2
— **Elizabeth Greene** – Kingston – "The Iron Shoes"
   – Poetry – ISBN – 978-1-897475-76-6
— **Richard Grove** – Brighton – "The Family Reunion" - 3rd Edition
   – Prose – ISBN – 978-1-897475-35-5
— **R.D. Roy** – Trenton – "A Pre emptive Kindness"
   – Prose – ISBN – 978-1-897475-80-3
— **Eric Winter** – Cobourg – "The Man In The Hat"
   – Poetry – ISBN – 978-1-897475-77-3

Second set of five books

— **Janet Richards** – Belleville – "Glass Skin"
   – Poetry – ISBN – 978-1-897475-01-0
— **R.D. Roy** – Trenton – "Three Cities"
   – Poetry – ISBN – 978-1-897475-96-4
— **Wayne Schlepp** – Cobourg – "The Darker Edges of the Sky"
   – Poetry – ISBN – 978-1-897475-99-5
— **Benjamin Sheedy** – Kingston – "A Centre in Which They Breed"
   – Poetry – ISBN – 978-1-897475-98-8
— **Patricia Stone** – Peterborough – "All Things Considered"
   – Prose – ISBN – 978-1-897475-04-1

Third set of five books

— **Mark Clement** – Cobourg – "Island In the Shadow"
  – Poetry – ISBN – 978-1-897475-08-9
— **Anthony Donnelly** – Brighton – "Fishbowl Fridays"
  – Prose – ISBN – 978-1-897475-02-7
— **Chris Faiers** – Marmora – "ZenRiver Poems & Haibun"
  – Poetry – ISBN – 978-1-897475-25-6
— **Shane Joseph** – Cobourg – "Fringe Dwellers" *Second Edition*
  – Prose – ISBN – 978-1-897475-44-7
— **Deborah Panko** – Cobourg – "Somewhat Elsewhere"
  – Poetry – ISBN – 978-1-897475-13-3

Forth set of five books

— **Diane Dawber** – Bath – "Driving, Braking and Getting out to Walk"
  – Poetry – ISBN – 978-1-897475-40-9
— **Patric Gray** – Port Hope – "This Grace of Light"
  – Poetry – ISBN – 978-1-897475-34-8
— **John Pigeau** – Kingston – "The Nothing Waltz"
  – Prose – ISBN – 978-1-897475-37-9
— **Mike Johnston** – Cobourg – "Reflections Around the Sun"
  – Poetry – ISBN – 978-1-897475-38-6
— **Kathryn MacDonald** – Shannonville – "Calla & Édourd"
  – Prose – ISBN – 978-1-897475-39-3

Single Anthology

"Changing Ways" A book of prose by Cobourg area authors including:
Jean Edgar Benitz, Patricia Calder, Fran O'Hara Campbell, Leonard
D'Agostino, Shane Joseph, Brian Mullally. **Editor: Jacob Hogeterp**
— ISBN – 978-1-897475-22-5